The warm-up

*For Françoise who said,"Why don't you
do a book about football called Goal!?"
And I said,"Hmm ..."*

First published in Great Britain by Andersen Press Ltd. in 1997.
First published in Picture Lions in 1999.

1 3 5 7 9 10 8 6 4 2

ISBN 0 00 664654-9

Picture Lions is an imprint of the Children's Division, part of HarperCollins Publishers Ltd
Text and illustrations copyright © Colin McNaughton 1997.
The author/illustrator asserts the moral right to be identified as the author/illustrator of the work.

Printed and bound in Singapore by Imago.

Colin McNaughton

PictureLions

An Imprint of HarperCollins*Publishers*

Preston is playing football in the garden one day

when his mum asks him
to go to the shop. Preston
decides to take his ball

and Preston, the world's most brilliant footballer, sets off.

He beats one player, then another, goes round the goalkeeper and shoots...

squash crunch trample

Manure

And the fans go wild:
"Ooh-ah-Preston Pig.
I said ooh-ah-Preston Pig!"

And Preston has the ball once more. He runs the whole length of the park and shoots…

It's a goal!

And the huge crowd chants:
"Preston, Preston,
He's the best 'un!"

And Preston goes looking for his hat-trick.

And this is incredible!
He's off on another run!
He goes round one. He goes
round two, three and he shoots...

It's a
goal!

That makes it three goals to nil,

but 'Super Preston' isn't finished yet!

He dribbles past the
great Pele, swerves past
the magical Maradona,

sweeps past Shearer,
puts the ball through the
legs of Ronaldo and shoots . . .

It's a goal!

Four-goal Preston sets off
home with the bread.

Mister Wolf leaves
the supermarket.

Mister Wolf takes a short cut
and lies in wait for Preston.

And Mister Wolf
gobbles Preston up.

Well, not really,
but that was his plan.

Extra time

COLIN MCNAUGHTON was born in Northumberland and had his first book published while he was still at college. He is now one of Britain's most highly acclaimed authors and illustrators of children's books and a winner of many prestigious awards, including the Kurt Maschler award in 1991.

Goal! is the fourth hilarious book featuring Preston the pig. The first, *Suddenly!*, was shortlisted for both the Smarties and the WH Smith/*SHE* Under-Fives awards. The third book in this series, *Oops!*, won the 1996 Smarties Book Prize in the under-fives category.

"A picture book of rare comic zest!"
Books for Keeps

"Don't miss this star player."
Evening Standard

*Look out for the next story
featuring Preston and friends,
to be published in Collins
Picture Lions in 2000.*